MY MOM MELTS ICE

BY JACKIE GONZALEZ   & HAMID YAZDAN PANAH

IMMIGRANT DEFENSE ADVOCATES 2021 ◉
ABOLISH ICE

THIS BOOK IS DEDICATED TO
EVERY MOTHER WHO SACRIFICES
TO MAKE THE WORLD A BETTER PLACE FOR EVERYONE

MY MOM HAS A SPECIAL JOB
THAT'S SORT OF HARD TO EXPLAIN
SHE WORKS WITH LOVE
AND CAN MAKE THE WORLD CHANGE

SHE USES HER LOVE
TO CHANGE THINGS FOR THE BETTER
MY MOM MELTS ICE
AND KEEPS FAMILIES TOGETHER

SHE DOESN'T DRESS UP
IN A COSTUME AND MASK
BUT SHE'S A SUPER HERO
WHO IS ALWAYS UP FOR THE TASK

WHEN PEOPLE MAKE A JOURNEY
TO A NEW COUNTRY LIKE OURS
MY MOM HELPS THEM ALONG
USING ALL OF HER POWERS

THERE ARE TIMES WHERE THE WORLD
CAN GROW COLD AND UNFAIR
AND IF YOU AREN'T CAREFUL
YOU CAN FALL INTO AN ICE LAIR

NO ONE WANTS TO BE
IN AN ICE LAIR ALONE
THEY NEED ALL THE HELP THEY CAN GET
TO FIND THEIR WAY HOME

MY MOM USES LOVE
AND FRIENDSHIP AND MIGHT
TO MELT THE ICE DOWN
AND BRING IN THE LIGHT

SHE WORKS WITH HER FRIENDS
AND PEOPLE IN THE COMMUNITY
SHE SPREADS HAPPINESS AND LOVE
AND FRIENDSHIP AND UNITY

SHE TURNS WALLS OF ICE
INTO RIVERS AND PONDS
WHERE WE CAN SPLASH AND PLAY
AND ALL GET ALONG

OUR WORLD IS BETTER
WITHOUT WALLS THAT DIVIDE
OUR LOVE AND HUMANITY
THAT WE ALL HOLD INSIDE

SHE USES HER VOICE,
HER HEART AND HER MIND
TO FIGHT FOR WHAT'S RIGHT
BY BEING SMART AND KIND

MY MOM IS A HERO
AND A FREEDOM FIGHTER
WHEN I GROW UP I HOPE
I CAN BE JUST LIKE HER

IMMIGRANT DEFENSE ADVOCATES (IDA) WAS FORMED IN 2020

THE MISSION OF IDA IS TO END POLICIES THAT DETAIN, DEHUMANIZE AND DESTROY IMMIGRANT COMMUNITIES

FIND OUT MORE AT IMADVOCATES.ORG

JACKIE GONZALEZ IS AN ATTORNEY AND MOM OF TWO AND ILLUSTRATED THIS BOOK. SHE HAS BEEN WORKING TO MELT ICE IN CALIFORNIA FOR OVER A DECADE. HER FAMILY IS ORIGINALLY FROM CUBA AND ARGENTINA, WHERE THEIR ICE STAYS IN THEIR DRINKS OR ON THEIR MOUNTAINS, WHERE IT BELONGS.

HAMID YAZDAN PANAH IS AN ATTORNEY AND WROTE THIS BOOK. HE IS AN IRANIAN REFUGEE AND RELOCATED TO THIS COUNTRY WHEN HE WAS 3. HE HOPES TO MELT ICE AND TRAVEL DOWN THE RIVERS TO UNCHARTED AND FREE OCEANS.

Made in the USA
Middletown, DE
05 May 2021